A Curious Chase

Bath New York Singapore Hong Kong Cologne Delhi Melbourne

Bath · New York · Singapore · Hong Kong · Cologne · Delhi · Melbourne

First published by Parragon in 2009

Parragon
Queen Street House
4 Queen Street
Bath BA1 1HE, UK

Adapted by Tim Webb
Illustrated by Disney Storybook Artists
Designed by Jerome Rebeiro
Printed and bound in Malaysia

A Curious Chase

Tim Webb

Once upon a time, a girl named Alice perched on a branch and daydreamed as her sister read aloud from a book. Try as she might, Alice couldn't concentrate. The day was simply too lovely to worry about a history lesson.

As her sister continued reading, Alice slipped away. 'If I had a world of my own, everything would be nonsense,' she told her kitten.

Suddenly, a rabbit in a waistcoat ran past. 'I'm late!' he cried as he looked at his watch.

At first, Alice thought nothing of this sight. But then she realised—rabbits don't wear waistcoats! Curious to know where he was heading, Alice chased after the strange creature. 'Mr Rabbit!' she called. 'Wait!'

But he darted into a rabbit hole.

Alice crawled into the rabbit hole and made her way through a dark burrow. But when she turned to speak to her kitten, she failed to see a hole in front of her.

Suddenly, Alice found herself falling. As she plummeted further down, the earthy walls transformed and strange items floated past.

Finally, Alice landed on a floor and spied the White Rabbit running down a hall. She followed, and reached a small room with a small door. Nearby, she found a bottle labelled 'Drink me'. As Alice drank the liquid, she shrank. But when she went to open the door, it was locked!

The key was on a table, far above Alice. The Doorknob suggested that she eat a cookie to grow. But when Alice ate the cookie, she grew too much!

Frustrated and confused, Alice started to cry. The room filled up with tears, and the Doorknob told Alice to drink from the bottle again. As the remaining liquid touched Alice's tongue, she shrank and landed in the empty bottle.

The bottle floated through the door's keyhole, taking Alice with it.

Alice sailed across deep water as she sat in the empty bottle. Eventually, she was washed up onto a beach, where a number of creatures were running in circles around a dodo in a purple coat. As Alice was swept up into the circle, she spied the White Rabbit nearby.

The White Rabbit promptly stood up, inspected his watch, and raced away from the shore. Alice took chase immediately, and followed him into the nearby woods.

As she peered through the trees, however, Alice lost sight of the White Rabbit. She also failed to notice two sets of eyes peering at her.

Suddenly, Alice turned and found herself face to face with a peculiar pair—two twins named Tweedledee and Tweedledum. Alice attempted to excuse herself, but the twins wouldn't let her leave! She explained that she was following the White Rabbit. 'I'm curious to know where he's going.'

'She's curious,' Tweedledum said to his brother. 'The oysters were curious, too.'

And so the twins told their story. 'The Walrus and the Carpenter,' began Tweedledee.

'Or the story of the curious oysters,' added Tweedledum.

One day, the Walrus and the Carpenter were walking on a beach. As the Walrus strolled along, discussing cabbages and kings, he spied an oyster bed that was full of young, playful oysters. He poked his head below the water and asked the oysters to follow him.

The oysters' mother didn't want her youngsters to go. But the little oysters were very curious about the world. They followed the Walrus.

As the Walrus talked to the little oysters, the Carpenter built a shack and heated up an oven. He wanted to cook them! But when he emerged from the kitchen, the Carpenter discovered that the Walrus had already eaten the oysters! Curiosity had brought about a bad fate.

'The end,' Tweedledee and Tweedledum said together.

Although she enjoyed the story, Alice was still curious about the White Rabbit. 'That's a very sad story,' she said, 'but I must go.'

And with that, Alice left Tweedledee and Tweedledum, and headed out of the woods. Soon, she reached a clearing where a little cottage stood. As Alice approached the cottage, the White Rabbit raced out. 'Mary Ann!' he shouted at Alice. 'Go get my gloves! I'm late!'

Alice crept inside to look for the White Rabbit's gloves. But when she reached his bedroom, she found a dish of cookies. As she took a bite from one, she grew and grew. Suddenly, Alice was so big that her arms and legs burst through the walls!

The Dodo and Bill, the chimneysweep, then walked past. They thought they could get Alice out by burning the house down!

Alice knew that this plan was far from good, so she plucked a carrot from the White Rabbit's garden and took a bite. Within moments, she shrank. But she shrank too much!

As she ran down the stairs and out of the cottage, Alice saw the White Rabbit running away. She tried to chase after him, but she was too small and too slow!

As Alice wandered to a nearby garden, she came across a caterpillar who was puffing on a pipe. 'Who are you?' he asked.

Alice explained that she wanted to be taller. 'Three inches is such a wretched height.'

The Caterpillar became very angry because he was three inches, too. 'It is a very good height, indeed!' he shouted as he surrounded himself with a swirl of smoke and disappeared.

Looking upwards, Alice saw that the Caterpillar had turned into a butterfly. As he flew away, he said, 'One side will make you grow taller, and the other side will make you grow shorter.'

'The other side of what?' Alice asked.

'The mushroom, of course!' he screamed in reply.

Alice reached down to the mushroom she was sitting on, and took two pieces—one from each side. As she bit into one piece, she grew and grew. Suddenly, her head burst out of the top of the trees!

Next, Alice bit the piece that she had grabbed from the other side of the mushroom. She shrank, and was tiny again.

In a final effort, Alice licked the 'tall side' of the mushroom. She returned to normal size, and put the leftover pieces in her pocket.

Alice continued walking and found herself in the woods once again. As she followed the nearby sound of singing, she arrived at a garden where a chaotic tea party was in progress. The Mad Hatter and the March Hare were sitting at the table, wishing each other a merry unbirthday.

Suddenly, the White Rabbit burst into the tea party. 'I'm so very, very late!' he cried.

The Mad Hatter grabbed the White Rabbit's watch. 'Well, no wonder you're late,' he said. 'Why, this clock is exactly two days slow.'

And with that, the Mad Hatter tried to fix the White Rabbit's watch. He dipped it in tea, ripped out its springs, and smeared food into it! The watch then started to jump about, so the March Hare smashed it. The pair then threw the White Rabbit out of their party!

With the White Rabbit gone, Alice slipped away from the party and headed back into the woods. But she soon became lost. Suddenly, she heard the voice of the Cheshire Cat.

'I'm through with rabbits,' Alice cried. 'I want to go home, but I can't find my way.'

'Naturally,' the Cheshire Cat answered. 'Always here, you see, are the Queen's ways.' Then he opened a secret door that led to a large castle.

As Alice walked through the door, she found herself in the castle's giant hedge maze. Turning this way and that, she stumbled upon three cards who were painting white roses red. She promptly asked what they were doing.

'Well, the fact is we painted the white roses by mistake, and the Queen—she likes them red,' one card explained.

And so Alice joined in and helped paint the roses.

All of a sudden, a trumpet sounded and a procession of cards formed a royal arch. The White Rabbit promptly raced through. 'Her Imperial Highness,' he announced, 'Her Grace, Her Excellency, Her Royal Majesty, the Queen of Hearts!'

The Queen entered with a serene smile on her face. But her smile soon disappeared when she saw paint dripping from a rose. 'Who's been painting my roses red?!' she bellowed. 'Off with their heads!'

When she spotted Alice, however, the Queen of Hearts forgot about her roses. 'Do you play croquet?' she asked.

Alice curtsied and replied, 'Yes, Your Majesty.'

The pair then started playing croquet. But during the game, the Cheshire Cat appeared and tangled the Queen's mallet in her skirt. As she swung, her skirt was pulled up and she fell over.

'Someone's head will roll for this,' the Queen shouted. Then she pointed at Alice. 'Yours!'

Within moments Alice was in the royal
court, with the White Rabbit reading the
charges against her: 'Teasing, tormenting ...
and thereby causing the Queen to lose her
temper.'

'Now, are you ready for your sentence?'
the Queen asked Alice.

'Sentence?' Alice replied. 'But there must
be a verdict first.'

'Sentence first!' the Queen bellowed back.
'Verdict afterwards.'

As the Queen continued screaming, Alice remembered that she still had two pieces of the mushroom that she'd eaten after meeting the Caterpillar. Alice quickly popped both pieces into her mouth, and started to grow. Soon she was towering over the Queen.

'Why, you're not a queen,' Alice said. 'You're just a fat, pompous, bad-tempered, old—' But before she could finish, Alice had shrunk back down to her regular size!

The Queen's blood quickly boiled. 'OFF WITH HER HEAD!' she screamed.

All of a sudden, Alice found herself being pounced on by the Queen's cards. She ran from the court and into the outdoor maze. She turned left and she turn right— she headed in every possible direction, cards chasing her along the way.

Before she knew it, Alice was back on the beach where she had landed after her trip in the bottle. She then saw the Caterpillar, who blew a large smoke ring at her. Within moments, the smoke had surrounded Alice.

As she looked back, she saw the Queen, the Mad Hatter, and many other creatures running after her.

Suddenly, Alice spotted the door in front of her. 'Still locked, you know,' the Doorknob said.

Alice leaped for the door. 'But the Queen,' she said. 'I simply must get out!' Then as she peered through the keyhole, she saw that she was already outside. She was asleep under the tree! 'Alice, wake up!' she cried.

Alice tossed and turned as she tried to awaken from her dream. Her cries then changed into another person's voice. 'Alice! Alice, will you kindly pay attention and recite your lesson?' her sister said.

Alice awoke with a start, and tried to tell her sister about the Caterpillar.

'Oh, for goodness sake. Alice ... Oh ... Come along. It's time for tea.'

The End.